I'd LOVE a Puppy

My sincere thanks to Karly Norton, Shadow Estate Boarding Kennels, Christchurch, New Zealand for her time, information, images and enthusiasm for this book.

Dear Reader

When I ask children what would be the best present for their birthday or for Christmas, many of them say: "I'd love a puppy!"

That's why I wanted to write about puppies. In this book, you'll learn about puppies and grown-up dogs, and discover whether or not they can talk!

WHAT'S THE BEST TEETH CARE FOR PUPPIES AND GROWN-UP DOGS? CHECK OUT PAGE 8 IN THIS BOOK.

Look at the checklist on page 5. It provides information to help people decide what kind of puppy might suit them.

In Chapter 6 you'll see where my dogs stay when I'm on holiday. Some dog kennels are like five-star hotels!

I hope you enjoy reading this book!

Sharon Parsons

For learning solutions, visit cengage.com.au

Contents

I'd Love a Puppy

1 A Puppy Report

TEXT TYPE
Information Report

A Puppy's First **Year** of **Life**

A dog is a puppy from birth to one year of age. That first year is an important time. The puppy must learn to live with its dog family, other animals, as well as humans.

"I'd love to play with you!"

"But I need lots of puppy training, too!"

Before you get a puppy, think about what kind of dog would suit your family and your home. Read this checklist to help you and your family decide.

Social Studies

Puppy Checklist

Male	or	Female
Large	or	Small
Short Hair	or	Long Hair
Pure Breed	or	Cross Breed
Active	or	Less Active
Inside Dog	or	Outside Dog
Buy a Puppy	or	Animal Shelter
Home Pet	or	Farm Dog
Good with Children		Clever

"Think about what I'll be like when I'm fully grown!"

VETS VACCINATE

A vet (or veterinarian) is an animal doctor. Vets care for farm animals, pets and wild animals. Vets give animals the right vaccinations to keep them healthy.

The **TOP Five** Ways to **Look After** a Puppy

puppy snuggles into bed

A Warm Bed for the Puppy

Like children, a puppy needs lots of sleep because it is still growing. Puppies love to snuggle into a soft bed with a rug to keep warm. Their beds should always be kept clean.

food for the puppy

Feed the Puppy

Most puppies need three small meals a day. A dog breeder or vet can provide advice about the best food for puppies. Puppies need plenty of clean water in a bowl.

training the puppy

Train the Puppy

Dogs like rules. In the wild, puppies learn how to behave from older dogs. In their new human home, puppies also need to learn some rules. One rule is not to chew things – like slippers.

exercise the puppy

No. 4

Exercise the Puppy

Puppies love to play. Exercise keeps them healthy and helps them grow strong. Exercise a puppy by taking it for short walks in the backyard, in a nearby park or along the street. When the puppy is older, it can go for longer walks.

Give the Puppy Lots of Cuddles!

When puppies are first born, they stay warm by cuddling up to their mother. Cuddles will comfort a new puppy and help it to feel safe in its new home. Children love the cuddles, too!

cuddles for puppy

A puppy that is well looked after will grow into a healthy, happy, well-trained dog. Pet dogs can become people's best friends.

Scientists have proven that people who own dogs live longer, happier and healthier lives.

Caring for the Puppy's Teeth

In the wild, puppies and dogs would have chewed on bones. So you should give them bones, too. Bones help keep the dog's teeth clean. Puppies and dogs should only be given raw bones. Cooked bones can splinter and cause stomach problems.

If you can't give your puppy or dog raw bones, use dog-chews or hard dog biscuits to help keep their teeth clean.

Doza is a British Bulldog. His two rows of teeth mesh together like sharks' teeth.

You may think giving your dog a bath is hard work. Think about how hard brushing its teeth would be! Some dogs that don't eat hard food will need to have their teeth cleaned. Vets use special brushes and toothpaste to clean the dog's teeth.

A puppy cleans its teeth by chewing on a bone.

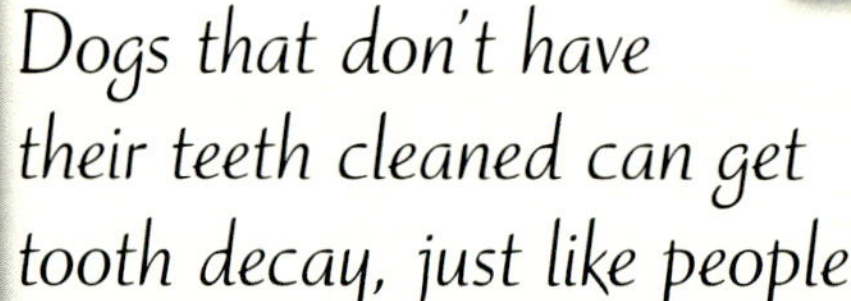

Dogs that don't have their teeth cleaned can get tooth decay, just like people.

2 Puppy Pre-School

I must not bark.
I must not bark.
I must not bark.
I must not bark.
I must not bark.

It's Time for **School**

Puppies should be trained by experts. At puppy pre-school, experts teach owners how to care for, and train, their puppies.

Puppies also learn how to:

- get along with other dogs and people
- learn commands, such as "come", "sit", "lie down" and "stay".

Stay

Puppy Owners Learn

Puppy pre-school classes help puppy owners to learn how to:

- train the puppy
- toilet-train the puppy
- stop problem puppy behaviour.

If we learn how to train a puppy, problem behaviour should stop.

sometimes accidents will happen

Q & A

Is it Normal for Dogs to Dig, Bark and Chew?

In the wild, dogs need to dig, bark and chew to survive. So it is normal for dogs to dig holes, bark and chew things.

New puppy owners need to teach puppies the rules about how to behave inside and outside their homes.

IN A PERFECT WORLD, EVERY DOG WOULD HAVE A HOME AND EVERY HOME WOULD HAVE A DOG!

Learn How to **STOP** Your **Puppy Jumping**

As puppies grow they become stronger and can jump very high. Excited puppies can look as if they have springs in their paws!

Why Puppies Jump Up

Puppies often greet other dogs by licking them. They want to greet people, too. They jump up and try to reach people's faces.

How to Stop Jumping

One way to stop puppies jumping up on people is to ignore the puppy when it jumps. Turn away from them. When the puppy stops jumping, reward it with a pat and a kind word. Ask a dog trainer for more advice.

Q & A

Can Fleas Jump Higher on Cats or Dogs?

In 2008, three French scientists found out that fleas jump higher on dogs than on cats!

a flea

3 Dig up Dog Facts

Dog Questions Are Answered

Q: Which dog cannot bark?

A: The only dog that cannot bark is the African wolf dog or basenji.

Q: Why might a dog have bad breath?

A: The dog may need its teeth cleaned. Or the dog may have gum disease.

Q: How many dog years are equal to one human year?

A: People have said that seven dog years was equal to one human year. But it depends on many factors, such as a dog's age, size, breed, gender and living conditions.

Q: When are "dog days"?

A: "Dog days" are summer's hottest days.

Q: What is the Dog Star?

A: The Dog Star is the brightest star in the sky. It is closest to our Sun. Its scientific name is Sirius.

Q: Where did dogs come from?

A: Dogs probably have the same ancestors as grey wolves.

Q: Multiple-Choice

What is ...

the tallest dog?

- Irish wolfhound
- Rottweiler
- Great Dane

the heaviest dog?

- Saint Bernard
- English mastiff
- German shepherd

the smallest dog?

- chihuahua
- Maltese terrier
- papillon

Famous Puppies

In England in 2009, a dog set a world record for giving birth to the largest number of puppies.

Tia, a bull-mastiff, had 24 puppies in one litter.

Usually there are six or seven puppies in a litter. Twenty-four is amazing!

bull-mastiff puppies

Social Studies

The President's Famous Puppy

In 2008, Barack Obama was elected President of the USA. During his acceptance speech, he told his two daughters, "You have earned the new puppy that's coming with us to the White House."

In April 2009, the girls met their new puppy. He is a Portuguese water dog called Bo. These dogs are very good at swimming and diving.

US President Barack Obama with his daughters, Malia and Sasha, and their dog Bo.

The Jobs Clever Dogs Do

Guide dogs help people who are blind or cannot see very well. Labrador retrievers are the most common guide dogs. There are three main colours – black, chocolate and yellow (cream to gold).

Benny the guide dog with Joan

Raising Guide Dogs

In Australia, Guide Dog Associations train these dogs. First, they ask puppy raisers to care for the puppies at their homes until they are 14 months old.

When the puppies go back to the Guide Dog Association, they have more training. Soon they are ready to guide their new owners.

Fritz the guide dog with Iain

"Detective" Dogs

People are not allowed to bring some things into the country, like plants, animals or drugs. Airport staff use clever dogs to detect or find these things in people's luggage.

a detector dog at an airport

Beagles and Labradors

Beagles and labradors are two of the most popular breeds to be used as detector dogs.

a trained beagle

Beagles and labradors make good detector dogs because they:

- have an excellent sense of smell
- have a calm nature in a busy airport
- are good with people.

What Happens to Airport Detector Dogs When They Retire?

Winstone and Melody were the first beagles to start detector work at Australian airports in 1992. Both dogs worked for eight years.

Winston sniffed over one million people. He retired to his handler's home in 2000.

Melody found many forbidden things. One was a live turtle! She moved to a retirement home for detector dogs.

5 Do Dogs Talk?

What Is Your **PUPPY** Trying to Communicate to You?

Dog owners have said that their dogs talk to them. But do puppies and dogs really talk?

Barking

Scientists tell us that dog barks mean different things. Researchers watch hours of videos of barking dogs. They record what the dogs are doing when they bark.

- **A noisy bark** means that a dog is upset, lonely or has heard something unusual.
- **A playful-sounding bark** means a dog is happy or wants to play.
- **An anxious-sounding bark** means a dog is worried.
- **A loud bark** tells others where a dog is.

Growling

Dogs also “talk” by growling. They may growl at another dog as a warning. A mother dog will growl to protect her puppies.

A dog’s growl can say, “Don’t come any closer” or “Stop!”

Whimpering

Dogs can also “talk” by whimpering. Whimpering is softer than growling or barking.

A whimper means that a dog is hurt, frightened or lonely. It can also mean the dog wants something.

Let’s Listen

Next time a puppy or a dog “talks”, listen carefully. See if you can understand what it’s saying.

We can be better puppy owners if we learn how to understand dog talk and dog behaviour.

“Woof! Woof! Woof!”

Dog *Senses*

SMELL

Dogs have a better sense of smell than people. It is about a million times better!

HEARING

Dogs have excellent hearing. They can also hear very high sounds that people can't hear.

TASTE

Humans have six times more taste buds than dogs. Dogs use their sense of smell to decide if food is good to eat.

SIGHT

Dogs cannot see colours as well as people. But dogs can see things better in dim light than people.

Language Arts and Communications

A Very Smart Dog

Imagine a dog that knows over 300 words. Betsy does. She is a Border Collie. Betsy proved she knew the words by finding things or doing things when she was asked.

Betsy lives in Austria.

Border Collie

TOUCH

Dogs like to be touched. They enjoy strokes, pats and cuddles. Always ask the owner before patting a dog.

6 A Hotel for Dogs

A Fun Place for Dogs While You're **Away**

Karly and her own dogs

Often people cannot take their dogs with them when they go on holiday. Many dogs go for their own holiday at a boarding kennel. It's like a hotel for dogs.

A Great Hotel for Dogs

Many dogs stay at Karly's Kennels in New Zealand. It's like a five-star hotel. Dogs love staying with Karly.

the entrance to Karly's kennels

Every Day is Fun

At the kennels, every day is fun for the dogs. Dogs are pack animals. The larger the pack, the more fun dogs have.

The Dogs' Menu

The dogs have two healthy meals a day, plus treats. Karly makes different meals for dogs that are on special diets and who are fussy eaters.

Fitness for Dogs

Dogs stay fit and healthy by playing and running around the paddocks on Karly's farm.

Karly says, "If we don't let the dogs play and run, they get very bored."

Doza and Nika play a tug-a-toy game.

"WE LOVE BUBBLE BATHS AT KARLY'S KENNELS!"

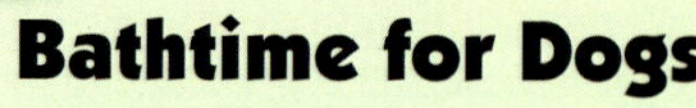

Bathtime for Dogs

Dogs can get dirty after running around and playing. Karly enjoys giving the dogs a bath and the dogs enjoy it, too!

Karly rides her bike around the paddock and the dogs love to chase her.

Social Studies

Dogs Can Fly!

Every day, dogs travel by plane between cities or countries. Pet travel companies help dog owners get the best care for their pets.

If your dog travels by plane, remember to:

- put their favourite toy or blanket inside the cage
- put water inside the cage
- give them a big cuddle before they fly.

Bibi waits in her travel cage.

Planes have warm, well-lit areas in the cargo hull for the animals' cages.

Pets are the last to board the plane and the first to be taken off the plane. Airport workers look after pets and other animals very carefully.

7 From Puppy to Senior Dog

A Dog's Life Stages

A puppy grows up in stages just like we do. Here are the main stages in a dog's life.

Truffles

PUPPY

Birth to Ten Days
The puppies' ears and eyes are shut. They cannot see or hear. Puppies must stay with their mother. Keep them warm.

10 to 14 Days
Puppies start to hear sounds. Their eyes open but they can't see very well yet.

3 to 5 Weeks
Puppies become active and want to explore. Like babies, they roll and crawl around.

Monty

5 to 12 Weeks
Puppies can now walk and explore further. They play with other puppies in the litter.

Puppies may go to their new home. They can start to be toilet trained and learn simple commands.

3 to 12 Months
Puppies will learn more commands, such as "sit", "down" and "stay". They should go to the toilet outside.

"TEENAGER" PUPPY

12 to 18 Months

The puppy is adult size. But it may still behave like a puppy. Keep reminding your dog how to behave!

PAWS

A dog's paws don't get bigger as they grow up.

ADULT DOG

1 ½ Years to 7 Years

The dog is settled into their home. Keep:

- feeding them healthy food
- putting clean water in their bowl
- giving them cuddles
- rewarding good behaviour
- taking them for walks every day
- playing games with them
- teaching them new commands.

Soots

Bibi

SENIOR DOG

From 7 Years to Old Age

By this age, dogs from some breeds need shorter, slower walks. They may need more regular visits to the vet to look after their health and their teeth.

Index

Glossary

cross breed	A dog with parents from two different types of dog, such as a labrador and a poodle (a labradoodle)
detector dogs	Dogs that are trained to find hidden objects, such as foods, drugs or explosives
dog breeder	A person who matches male and female dogs of the same breed so that their puppies will be that breed too.
gender	The sex of an animal, either male or female
mesh	Fitting together closely
pure breed	A dog with parents that are both the same type of dog (such as labradors)
retriever	A type of hunting dog that has been bred and trained to locate and fetch prey such as ducks or rabbits
scientific name	The Latin name given by scientists to living things to help classify them in a system everyone understands